Lockdown Lullabies

Ian D Francis

Lockdown Lullabies

DEDICATION

To Prof, LJ and Wednesday Girl

And to the many heroes of Covid who have cared for, nursed, protected, taught, delivered, fed, listened, helped and supported

Lockdown Lullabies

CONTENTS

Lockdown Lullabies

ACKNOWLEDGMENTS

To all those who have inspired these works, some knowingly and others completely unaware.

Lockdown Lullabies

Wednesday Girl

If Roses are red
Then why are these white
Be bad
Be good
Be Wednesday night
Love won't grow
If left by itself
So rush to my side
And kiss my mouth
Soft with passion
Hard with desire
Adrenalin rush
Like a walk on a wire
Burning like
A forest fire
More elegant
Than cathedral spires
Delicate
And yet so strong
She lays beside me
All night long
And when my inspiration
Is all but gone
Be bad
Be good
Bring Wednesday on

The End of a Perfect Day

It's the end of a perfect day
The sun sets in a blood red sky
It's the end of a perfect day
She whispers a final goodbye

It's the end of a perfect day
No Jewels in the night time sky
It's the end of a perfect day
All he can say is why?

It's the end of a perfect day
But at least they'll still be friends
It's the end of a perfect day
We all know how that one ends

It's the end of a perfect day
The sun sets in a blood red sky
It's the end of a perfect sky
Never again to rise

Jack-off TV

I've been hammered
I've been screwed
Raped and abused
Detained and restrained
With my head in a noose
I've been spit roast
Served up on toast
For the Father Son and Holy Ghost
I've texted
I've sexted
I'm fast and I'm loose
I've smiled at the lens
Played lesbian friends
Simulating pleasures
That just never end
So look into the camera
Look deep into my eyes
And you can pretend
It's my hand in your flies
On your mobile
Your TV
And laptop device
We've got Asian babes
Under age
And bored readers wives
So, come dial up my number
Talk dirty to me
Pretend that we're lovers
On Jack-off TV

It's not the career
I had in mind you see
But if the money's right honey
It's good enough for me
I'm a working girl
I've come out to play
A temptress by night
And a mother by day
I feed my kids
I pay my dues
So, dial up my number
I'll bend over for you
Just key in the details
Of your credit card
This love is for sale
It's no holds barred
So, come dial up my number
Talk dirty to me
Just don't tell your mother
She'll think it's obscene
Forsaking no others
You know what I mean
Pretend that we're lovers
On Jack-off TV

My Way

And now the end is near
And so I face my last venetian
I've lived a life that's short
And as it speeds
Towards completion
I think
Well what the fuck
I curse my luck
And scream expletives
And soon
Before you know
I'll be deleted

I've hitched and stowed away
As I travelled along
Life's lonely highway
The dead ends
And hairpin bends
That lead me back
Back home to nowhere
I've lived a life of pain
But then again
Well what else is there
And all
All through the years
I really don't care

Regrets
I've had a million
And a million more
Of which I'm not sure
The wheels of injustice turn
And what I've learned
Is not worth knowing
The reports of my demise
Are full of lies
That just keep flowing
And when
You're knee deep in shit
Well just keep going

Yes, there were times
I'm sure you knew
When I drank meths
And Special Brew
I filled my cup
Then threw it up
Down on my knees
Down on my luck
The band plays the blues
I hit the snooze
And did it my way

Tinsel Town

The rain beat hard and soaked the ground

We waved goodbye to Tinsel town

By the swollen river she lay me down

And placed upon my head a crown

And there I met the king

Life's a Bitch

Around her porcelain neck my fingers curl
This battered woman was once a girl
Squeeze until her lips turn blue
Because life's a bitch
And I'm one too

Crush her heart and steal her youth
The stone cold lies and brutal truth
The body lives, the spirit dies
Because life's a bitch
And so am I

Suck the life from her veins
Take her beauty give her pain
Tie her naked to the tree
Because life's a bitch
Just like me

A brand-new start the same old shit
Nothing ever comes of it
She'll never reap the love she sows
Because life's a bitch
Don't you know?

Hide your face beneath the covers
We were never really lovers
Pretty soon you will discover
That life's a bitch
And so's my mother

Your mother left without a word
The needle that your dad preferred
The child that you will never hold
Because life's a bitch
Or so I'm told

Did you ever really stand a chance?
A victim of your circumstance
Old before she reached her youth
Because life's a bitch
Aint that the truth

From midwife to the undertaker
Pretty soon you'll meet your maker
You'll never have the final laugh
Because life's a bitch
I think I'll pass

One day when you least expect
You'll gaze upon the lives I've wrecked
Their numbers stretch from here to hell
Because life a bitch
Can't you tell?

Kicks Like A Mule

Well I used to be a sentimental fool
That believed all you need is love and that love will conquer all
But I soon found to my cost that life is sick and cruel
And it batters and it bruises, and it kicks like a mule

Well I'm looking at you and you are standing there
With the stars in your eyes and the moonlight in your hair
And it's all that I can do to just stand and stare
And you're smiling back at me and I wonder if I dare

Pinch myself in case I wake up
Because this cannot be my life because my life has always sucked
And when you hit rock bottom and you're down on your luck
Well it smacks you in the jaw like a ten-ton truck

See these scars here upon my wrists
Everyone is a failure shall I write you a list
Put and gun to my head but somehow I missed
Cos I've never known love and I've never been kissed

And I wish that I could find the words to say
How I feel this very minute how I'm feeling this day
So I drop to my knees and I plead and I pray
That you will never leave me and you'll never go away

I still remember the very first time
When you said that I was yours and you said that you were mine
And that we'd be together until the end of time
Brought a tear to my eye and a shiver down my spine

But nature gripped me and made me hesitate
So you brushed my face a told me that you would always wait
A chance such as this a man should not waste
And perhaps I'll never know just how good you taste

Today the birds brought me the news
That you're stood before the preacher and about to say I do
So I jumped upon my motorbike and like the wind I flew
And you're standing at the alter all borrowed and blue

And a choir of angels call out your name
And they're singing our song and they sing it once again
And you're running down the aisle and you're moving like a train
And we don't need words we don't need to explain

There's a look of shock among the wedding guests
As run out of the church and you're throwing off your dress
Don't know where we're going don't know how far we'll get
We just jump on my bike and ride to the sunset

Now I can't express how happy we are
When we're making love and you're lying in my arms
Then we count all our blessings and we count all the stars
And this thing that we have they don't sell it in jars

The years went past and then the sickness came
You broke all your promises when the angels called your name
And I'm left here all alone now since you went away
And I'd give up my life just to hold you once again

Well I used to be a sentimental fool
That thought all you need is love and that love will conquer all
But I soon found to my cost that life is sick and cruel
That it blisters and bruises and kicks like a mule

Wild Orchids

You walk naked through the wilderness
Among the grasses and the leaves
If we were wild orchids
Then darling I would see
Your voluptuous body
Glistening in sweat
Your soft perfect lips
A deep crimson red
But I am not a flower
Nor a bird or a bee
I am shackled and I am chained
So I guess I'll never see
You walk naked through the wilderness
Without boundary or fence
And your silky-smooth moisture
Will never ever quench
My thirst or my hunger
Like the flower I must die
But your beauty lives forever
Naked and wild
Without you life is nothing
Without you I am lost
Like the orchid in winter
I am bitten by the frost
So you can buy and sell me
When all is said and done
But tell me wild orchid
Tell me when you come

When the gods laid eyes upon you
You captured their hearts
The sun woke the sleeping clouds
The moon and the stars
Constellations welcomed you
The northern lights shone
I reached out to touch you
But already you were gone
Now I cannot compete with gods
Or turn back time
This World keeps on turning
And you are not mine
So you can buy and sell me
When all is said and done
But tell me wild orchid
Tell me when you come

The Boy Who Never Came Home

It was July twenty four when the boy went to war
The poor lad didn't know what he was fighting for
But the sergeant said son we'll soon settle this score
And we'll all be home before

The Christmas lights sparkle and shine
And the church bells ring out their chimes
And the ladies are looking so fine
And smiling at you.

The boy felt afraid as his comrades were slain
Beaten and butchered and wounded and maimed
The bullets did whistle, and the shells did rain
Until a shiny grey bayonet sent him to his grave

Now the Christmas lights sparkle and shine
And the church bells ring out their chimes
And the ladies with tears in their eyes
Are crying for you.

Now he lays in the garden alone
Where the flowers are only of stone
And the soil's a tangle of bones
The boy who never came home

If Only Tonight I Could Sleep

If only tonight I could sleep
In the moon light
And the stars
If only tonight I could lie
In the safety of your arms
Then I could sleep
Then I could dream

If only tonight I could sleep
Underneath a big old tree
That stands upon a hill
Which tumbles to the sea
In the safety of your arms
I could sleep
I could dream

If only tonight I could sleep
In a meadow of wild flowers
In the sun kissed warmth of an autumn day
I could lie for hours
In the breeze the grass would gently sway
And softly whisper your name
If I were safely in your arms
Then I could dream again

Ugly

Ugly woman
Mink coat
Forty beautiful lives
Died in the cage where they spent their days
Vanity has its price

Powdered rhino gives you the horn
Canadian clubbed seals on ice
Their pathetic squeals ask
Why was I ever born?
Vanity has its price

Dead Leaves (2)

No once upon a time
No happy ever after
Just a nobody
Nobody's father

And his babies are washed away
Like dead leaves down the drain
And his babies are washed away
Like dead leaves

He can see in your eyes
He can see it in your face
He's taking up your time
Invading your space

So he'll go away now
Disappear without trace
Cos he know what he is
And he knows his place

So no once upon a times
No happy ever after
I guess he's just a nobody
Nobody's father

And his dreams are washed away
Like litter in the street
And his unborn babies cry
They haunt him when he sleeps

And his dreams are washed away
Like dead leaves down the drain
And his babies are washed away
Like dead leaves

The American

Please allow me to introduce myself
I'm a man who needs no introduction
I own this land you stand upon
Acquired by theft, deception and corruption
I claimed the crown to Washington
In an undemocratic election
I bought my votes with dollar notes
And just a little help from the Kremlin

I loathe the whores who question gun laws
And my stance on global warming
I have a plan for Rocket man
So take this as a warning
For I'll declare war like never before
With my weapons of mass destruction
And if BLM protest by peaceful means
I'll crush them without hesitation

I spit in the eye of the FBI
When they investigate my scandals
The deafening silence of hush money
From my old flame Stormy Daniels
I'll build my wall strong and tall
To halt the southern invasion
While the racist finger upon the trigger
Hides behind the Fifth Amendment

So please allow me to introduce myself
I'm the king of all I survey
The trees upon the far-off hill
The fishes down in the bay
The sun the sea the sand the sky
The people I represent
I'll destroy them all should I feel inclined
Because I'm The President

Angels and Guitars

Maybe it was ignorance
Perhaps it was neglect
But at times like these I find it best
To remain tight lipped and reflect
Upon the inadequacies of other men
From Saddam to St Paul
And eventually I'll convince myself
It wasn't my fault after all

Some days when I wake up
The world seems very small
I look around this empty room
Then curl up in a ball
I think about what might have been
If I hadn't been so weak
The tears hang heavy upon the pillow
As I cry myself to sleep

I remember the day we met
The angels sang our song
I picked up my guitar
And I tried to play along
But the angel wasn't Gabriel
But the black angel of doom
Your singing was off key that day
And my guitar was out of tune

We walked hand in hand
Just like lovers do
Upon the banks of the old canal
What you saw in me I never knew
The idiot boy that smiled at you
You gave a second glance
A chancer such as him
Didn't need a second chance
I watched you slip into his arms
It all but broke my heart
Then you gave to him your innocence
Because he could play guitar

Death by Fitting Room

Some questions are really best left unanswered
Some mysteries are best unsolved
Some puzzles are better left never completed
Some stories are better untold
But since man learned to walk on his own two feet
Never too proud to fall
The female species remains a mystery
And the answer has alluded them all
Great minds have tried, and great minds have failed
Einstein himself mused
Stephen Hawkins theorised but very quickly realised
He was totally confused
So men such as I have no response
But the interrogation persists
Their tormentors demand an answer
'Does my bum look big in this?'

The condemned are shackled by shopping bags
Amidst the gathering gloom
The executioner prepares the noose
Its death by fitting room

I'm not sure of much about anything
But of this I'm absolutely certain
The wrath of a million calories
Will be unleashed when she draws back the curtain

Minutes drag and time stands still
Then finally success
Against the laws of physics
She squeezes into the dress

Well she's stretched and strained
And bitched and complained
But the mirror still deceives her
She's cut the seams used Vaseline
And a pair of tyre levers

And as she exits the fitting room
Let me sign my own death wish
Then she looks at me with hopeful eyes and says
'Does my bum look big in this?'

Should I lose myself amongst the crowds
Disappear into the throng
I'm not sure which answer I should give
But I know it will be wrong

Panic fills my every thought
The colour drains from my cheeks
My palms are sweating my mouth is dry
I've lost the will to speak

The finally some inspiration
'Well perhaps just a little tight'
But an honest opinion was not required
There'll be no sex tonight!

I'm a dead man walking in Debenhams
House of Fraser has sealed my fate
Then she looks at me with tearful eyes and says
Pass me a size twenty-eight.

I'm S – H – O – PP – I – N – G
In Top Shop Gap and Monsoon
At Principles and Pineapple and Kookai
It's death by fitting room.

Lies

There a story that needs to be told
But it's not one that you'll want to hear
So, turn away
Save your ears
For you will surely break down and cry
At the harsh reality
And the brutality
Of my life

There's a fire burning in my chest
And it rages and roars like a furnace
And its flame
Never dies
It is fueled by your cruelty and lies
And your lies
And your lies

My god, why did you desert me?
My god, what have you done?
You said you never wanted to hurt me
You said you only wanted some fun
But I'm not laughing
Not even a smile
No, I'm not laughing
I am dirty
And worthless
And vile

And so, the story goes on
But no one ever really knows
The nights I spent on my knees
Praying only to please you
These hands that have relieved you

Of your suffering
And your lies
And your lies and your lies and your lies

It was you put my head in this noose
From my gallows I ask what's the use
Of apologies
And excuses
And lies

A Thousand Nights

According to the holy scriptures of the Seventh Day Adventist
Or was it Karen Brady on a repeat episode of The Apprentice
Then again it might have been the stranger I met in the waiting
room of the dentist
But whoever it was who said it I don't believe a single word

I've forgotten much more than I choose to remember
That Guy Fawkes is the reason for fireworks in November
I've forgotten that life is just one great big adventure
And I don't believe in Santa Claus anymore

But I can't forget the night we spent together
Or the thousand nights that we have spent apart
You told me it was fate and I believed you
As I held you close I heard the beating of your heart

There's no such thing as fate as I discovered
And all the doctors agree that I will never recover
In that moment I thought that we would always be lovers
It's funny how your dreams can seem so real

The party's in full swing as I head to the station
But I'm not sure why we're here or if we're celebrating
A wedding, birthday, anniversary or coronation
A funeral, wake, burial, embalming or cremation

But I can't forget the night we spent together
Or the thousand nights that we have spent apart
You told me it was fate and I believed you
As I held you close I heard the beating of your heart

Lockdown Lullabies

The mail train arrived and has long since departed
There were no letters or cards from you and no parcels
I've always believed in finishing what I started
Like food waste you scraped me from your plate

And I never sleep although I feel so very tired
The caffeine coursing in my veins keeps me wired
I hope life brings you all your heart desires
My love is so much stronger than my hate

But I can't forget the night we spent together
Or the thousand nights that we have spent apart
You told me it was fate and I believed you
As I held you close I heard the beating of your heart

The Aftershock

I opened up a bar at the turn of the year
Selling hard liquor and ice-cold beer
With a fear of love and love of fear
And if you've had a good time
Well you sure aint had it here

I hired forty maids to serve behind the bar
Burlesque beauties in a push-me-up bra
And a guitar man with a one string guitar
He sings like the devil in a heavenly choir

But it's the happiest of hours at the Aftershock
Where the bar never closes and the door never locks
And the bar room clock tick tock tick tock
Tick tock
Tick tock
Tick tock

The slightest of hands in five card stud
Slapping down dollars with a menacing thud
The stakes are high when you pay with blood
The dealer has a thirst he just can't get enough

There's sawdust on the floor and smoke fills the air
If you've a story to tell boy then pull up a chair
Drink away your troubles son because nobody cares
And if the law comes a calling I'll make you disappear

But it's the happiest of hours at the Aftershock
Where the bar never closes and the door never locks
And the bar room clock tick tock tick tock
Tick tock
Tick tock
Tick tock

Live every day as if it was your last
The answer you seek is in the bottom of a glass
Name your pleasure sir you only have to ask
But time keeps on moving so you'd better make it fast

The money that you owe is more than you can pay
Sink another round it doesn't matter anyway
Sold your soul to the bottle and gave your sobriety away
Now you're stuck inside the Aftershock until your dying day

But it's the happiest of hours at the Aftershock
Where the bar never closes and the door never locks
And the bar room clock tick tock tick tock
Tick tock
Tick tock
Tick tock
Tick tock
Tick tock
Tick tock
Tick tock
Tick tock

Lucy Jones

Pretty Lucy Jones lay sleeping on the sand
A freshly picked flower in her tiny little hand
Her skin was whiter than the driven snow
Wake up Lucy it's time to go

She didn't know a single soul
The saddest story that was ever told
She went to the city in search of fun
Heaven knows she found none

She couldn't keep up with her pretty little self
Afraid of being left on the shelf
Life's a gamble any ways
Grew tired of all those lonely days

But that's not where the story ends
Couldn't find a single friend
She'd have been better off all alone
Stay home Lucy, Lucy stay home

She grew up in a one-horse town
The one horse died now it's not around
She dreamed of the ocean that she'd never seen
Wild and wonderous and emerald green

Her mother drank her days away
Her daddy never replied from jail
No cards or letters did he send
That's not where the story ends

A small black case was all she took
Two pretty dresses and a dog-eared book
Not much to show for her fifteen years
Beware Lucy, Lucy beware

She hitched a ride out of no-horse town
Caught a train as the sun went down
Riding into a red sunset
She thought to herself, no regrets

She looked for the streets that were paved with gold
Just the way that dreams are sold
But dreams are real only when you sleep
Poor Lucy was in too deep

She woke up in the morning rain
Watched the water run down a dirty drain
In that moment she saw her life
Oh Lucy dry your eyes

Well you can check out but you can never quit
Her mama told her just get on with it
Good advice was in short supply
Oh my Lucy, Lucy oh my

Then one day she met someone
Perhaps she said he was the one
For every girl there is a boy
She was overcome with joy

He held out his hand and softly smiled
Said hey pretty girl let's walk a while
We'll walk to the shore of this old land
Lucy took his giant hand

Well Lucy said it's a dream come true
To see the ocean wild and blue
But wake up Lucy from your dream
Not everything is what it seems

She squeezed the strangers' giant hand
As she stood there laughing on the golden sand
The best day of her life by far
When the sun went down they counted stars

She was pure and never been kissed
She closed her eyes and pursed her lips
He held her tightly in his arms
Lucy succumbed to his masculine charms

And there he gently lay her down
Picked wild flowers from the stony ground
She was so happy she almost burst
He would be her very first

The greatest love story ever wrote
She softly sighed as he caressed her throat
His big hands tightened like a noose
You can struggle Lucy but it's no use

The stranger rose and headed north
The sea raged against the shore
Life goes on just as before
Poor Lucy breathed no more

Pretty Lucy Jones lay sleeping on the sand
A freshly picked flower in her tiny little hand
Her skin was whiter than the driven snow
Wake up Lucy it's time to go

Trouble

Hey man well he aint no brother
You're just another bad-ass mother
I wish there was somewhere I could run for cover
Trouble's coming and its heading straight for me

Hey girl well she aint no sister
God knows I can't resist her
Her ruby lips and her ice-cold kisses
Love is coming and its heading straight for me

Her daddy told me if I ever touch her
He'll blow the head clean off my shoulders
He's got a shotgun and a Colt revolver
A bullet's coming and its heading straight for me

Sheriff Law told me to leave town boy
If you stay I'm gonna take you down boy
Good advice shouldn't be ignored boy
The Law is coming and its coming after me

Think I'll go to the One-Eye Saloon
The men fight and the ladies swoon
The piano plays but it's out of tune
Whiskey pours and it pours all night for me

I stagger home as the day is dawning
And when I wake sometime next morning
On my pillow is writ a warning
Hell is coming and its heading straight for me

The devil may care but god she sure don't
I packed my bags and wrote goodbye notes
Before they put a noose around my sweet throat
Death is coming and he's carrying a hood and rope

I tried to run but I didn't get far
A state trooper outside of Wichita
Cuffed my hands in the back of a police car
A judge is coming and its judgement day for me

Judge Cooper said how do you plead
You're charged with love in the first degree
My fiery lover screamed set my man free
Love is coming and its heading straight for me

Trouble town is where I made my home
Trouble town is where they'll lay my bones
Where people come just to read my stone it reads
Here lays Trouble and Trouble was his middle name

Secrets

The secrets
That you're keeping
I hear them
As you're sleeping
You cry out
In your sleep
Some secrets
You can't keep
And your secret
Is a secret
No more

When the moon shines
Up above
You dream of
Forbidden love
And in the morning
When you wake
The smile that you smile
It is fake
A well composed lie
Exposed by
Mistake

The detail
Of your betrayal
An unspoken
Masquerade
I ask you
How you feel
These feelings
Are not real
So unfaithful
But I'm not hateful
No way

Such beauty
Fades away
One by one
Our hair will turn to grey
Someday
You'll walk beside the sea
The waves will whisper
You should leave
As you discover
Your new lovers
Secret

A secret
Concealed
Never spoken
Nor revealed
It will eat away
At your soul
A secret
Never told
And on your death bed
Words left unsaid
Die with you

The Debt

Lucifer said as he drew his last breath
Did we make a deal do you owe me a debt?
Were you hoping that I would forget
For the wealth that you hold
Do you owe me your soul?
It's time my friend
I'm here to collect

The Man Who Has It All

When he kissed her for the first time
Her lips tasted just like honey
He wanted to send flowers
But he didn't have much money
So he put his pen to paper
And tried to find the words
But the only thing that he could write
Was I love you Wednesday girl

Days spent doing nothing
Just walking hand in hand
And the sound of waves crashing
Against the shoreline of this land
Lying under willow trees
And watching clouds roll by
He's waited for you Wednesday girl
And he'll love you until he dies

Beauty is a fickle mistress
Her allegiance but a fleeting glance
The soft caress of her perfect skin
Every time they danced
Drift towards unconsciousness
The perfume of her hair
When Wednesday girl came around
He was just happy to be there

Sail away to the Isle of Swes
Just drinking tea and giving head
Lying naked on the unmade bed
Nowhere he'd rather be instead
And when it came to say goodbye
A kiss to keep him warm at night
Intoxicated by loves allure
Until Wednesday came around once more

Like horses running wild and free
Or a hurtling diesel train
A fire burns within his heart
Adrenaline through his veins
A stroll along the high wire
No net to break his fall
Without a penny to his name
He's the man who has it all

When Love is Not Enough

What happens when the honeymoon ends
And all that's left is love
When the thrills slowly fade away
And love is not enough

The wedding march grinds to a halt
The guests have all gone home
A couple walking hand in hand
Each walking all alone

What happens to the fairytale
And happy ever after
What happens to all the good times
When tears are not of laughter

What happens when you're just good friends
And you cannot feel the rush
What happens when the romance ends
And love is not enough

A Right Royal Mess

Harry and Wills, Megan and Katie
They haven't been getting along too well lately
Big brother Billy gave H some advice
About the royal suitability of his Hollywood wife
But the beardy ginger prince he was none too pleased
Now he lives in a palace in Los Angeles

Charlie boy he's the king in waiting
But Liz don't look like abdicating
With steroids and drugs and surgery
She's going to live to a hundred and eighty
Just hanging around for your anointment
Is just one of life's little disappointments

Wills is a chip off his father's block
But looking at H well I'm not too sure
There's rumour and scandal and a theory
That all that's royal is not royalty
Best let that sleeping corgi be
And not fan the flames of conspiracy

The Grand Old Duke took early retirement
When talking to the Feds became a legal requirement
A betrayal of trust and abuse of power
And (alleged) paedo parties at Epstein Towers
Perhaps one day we'll know the truth
Behind the car crash BBC interview

The rest of them well I don't have time
For those that are paid just to wait in line
For a throne that they know will never be theirs
With a view of the world that nobody shares
Try getting a job and paying some taxes
And relieve the burden on the struggling masses

But I'm not pushing for a federal state
I just wish sometimes you'd reign it in mate
Millions wasted on royal weddings
Could go a long way to house the homeless
A national treasure gotten out of hand
We only need one royal to rule this land

The Well

The well has run dry
But her thirst remains
She wants to be free
Break free of the chains
The boy she once knew
Has taken the train
To anywhere but here
Now she prays for the rain

So let the skies open
Until she's soaked to the skin
Thunder and lightning
Until her body is cleansed
There's a feeling inside her
That the stranger beside her
Is the boy she once knew
Before love denied her

Teacher

Jack was excited to be starting school, he'd woken early and put on his uniform for the first time, he felt very grown up, way beyond his five years…

The teacher said to the boy, what do you want to do with your life
Let me give you some advice
He shared his wisdom and explained the facts
According to his ideology
Work hard, study hard, try hard
Respect your teachers and listen to what they tell you
Then you will pass

The boy thought about this advice and then returned to the original question, he said
"I'll tell you what I want to do with my life
I want to be happy
I want to see and experience new things
I want to be free
I want to have fun
But most of all I want to live"

He turned to the teacher and said
"What do you want to do with your life, and why did you become a teacher?"

The teacher replied I studied hard
At school I was always in the top sets
The top sets had the best teachers and the best teachers got the best results
Everybody passed

Age five to eleven in the classroom, in my bedroom, books, notes, essays Maths, English, Science, all that good stuff

I studied and revised
Remembering stuff, facts, figures, formulas
Read my notes
Learned by rote

Passed the test
And went to a top secondary school

"What happened then?" the boy asked

At secondary school I was always in the top sets
The top sets had the best teachers and the best teachers got the best results
Everybody passed
Age eleven to 16 in the classroom, in my bedroom, books, notes, essays, Maths, English, Science, all that good stuff
I studied and revised
Remembering stuff, facts, figures, formulas
Read my notes
Learned by rote
Passed the test
And went into school sixth form

"And then what?"

In sixth form I was always in the top sets
The top sets had the best teachers and the best teachers got the best results
Everybody passed

Age sixteen to eighteen in the classroom, in my bedroom, books, notes, essays Maths, English, Science, all that good stuff
I studied and revised
Remembering stuff, facts, figures, formulas
Read my notes
Learned by rote

Passed the test
And went to a top university

"I think I'm getting the gist of this said the boy, "but just in case what happened at university?"

At a top university you have the best teachers
The best teachers got the best results
Everybody passed
Age eighteen to twenty-one in the classroom, in my bedroom, books, notes, essays Maths, English, Science, all that good stuff
I studied and revised
Remembering stuff, facts, figures, formulas
Read my notes
Learned by rote
Passed the test
And graduated
I was so thrilled to be through with study that I threw my mortar board in the air

"And then what did you do?"

I did another year's study on teacher training as I wanted to teach children and help them learn

The boy paused for a moment and asked, "so what did you learn from all this studying"

The teacher drew a breath and began Maths, English, Science, all
that good stuff
Revision
Remembering stuff, facts, figures, formulas
Reading notes
Learn by rote
And how to pass the test

"But what of happy, but what of free, but what of fun, but what of
living, what did you *actually* learn" said the boy only this time a
little more insistent

The teacher scratched his head

Fast Food Folsom Prison Blues

I see my food a coming
Chips and burgers that I crave
I hear them pushing buttons
On the microwave
Oh I know I have it coming
I can smell those greasy snacks
But if I don't change my diet
I'll have a heart attack

I bet there's big folk eating
In fast food burger bars
Their probably drinking coffee
And eating chocolate bars
Well you know I don't go running
My drinks aren't sugar free
So I get the table service
To save my energy

When I was a young boy
My mama told me son
Always go ciabatta
Don't have the seeded bun
But I ordered one in Reno
With a side of fries
And when I bite into that gristle
I hang my head and cry

Well I'm a fast food lover
Heading for an early grave
Don't bother with me brother
I'm not looking to be saved
I ignore all the warnings
Right before my eyes
I'm not counting up the calories
I'm going supersize

Lockdown Lullaby

If you see me standing at a distance
Waiting in a line
Could be I'm waiting for a vaccine brother
Could be I'm biding my sweet time
Mask up kids and sanitize
Don't risk old granny's life
Because when you mess with Mother Nature daddy
Your children pay the price

Tier one
God bless your mortal soul

Tier two
Stockpile the toilet roll

Tier three
Don't stand so close to me

Tier four
Stay home and lock your door

Tier Pfizer
Hope is on its way

Tier six
Don't let the households mix

Tier minus seventy

Tier eight
Mutate mutate mutate

Tier nine
God save the NHS

Tier ten
From this U-Turn Government

Hey Folks

Hey folks...
I've been thinking
And I'd like to share my thoughts with you

Sometimes when you walk through the garden of gloom
It's easy to miss that the world is in bloom
And if you only view the world from your living room
Then you need to change your view mate

So stop moaning about the posters and the words on the stairs
And the tick-tock of the clock and how life's not fair
Raise your head up son and be more aware
Of the black cloud that you are towing

Teacher what's my lesson let me drink from the fountain
Preacher preach your sermon of Muhammed and the mountain
Miracles can happen if you only believe
But if you've nothing good to say then perhaps you should leave

You hoover up the mood with your miserable glare
Bring gloom to the room with your stories of doom
And if the grass is much greener way over there
I'll order you a taxi and I'll pay for the fare

So stop moaning and groaning and blaming the world
Try giving it a rest or try giving it a whirl
Try finding some words that are positive and kind
For everything that's wrong in your tiny little mind

And if you just stopped moaning I think you would agree
That the best things in life they really are free
Like the dawning of the day and the birds and the bees
And how from tiny acorns grow mighty oak trees

So tomorrow when you wake up and you watch the sunrise
Remember that life is the jackpot prize
So find some kind words for a passerby
And thank your lucky stars that you're alive

Daddy's Little Girl

When you're feeling uncertain
In an uncertain world
I will be your daddy
You'll be daddy's little girl

A Dear Old Friend of Mine

A dear old friend of mine
She visits now and then
We sit and talk a while
And then she's gone again
I plead that I may go with her
But she says it's not my time
I pray that she will take me soon
This dear old friend of mine

Last night when she called on me
My question was the same
To take me with her when she goes
So I may be free again
Give me back some dignity
I take thee as my wife
And I shall be so glad to go
With a dear old friend of mine

And as I lay and watched the sun
Rise above the trees
My lover came and took my hand
And gave me sweet release
Now I lay among the flowers
Beneath an ancient vine
As happy as the summer breeze
With a dear old friend of mine

The Idiot Puppeteer

Such a sad little girl
So mad at the world
With her ringlets and curls
She's so pretty

Such an angry little child
Rattled and riled
She wants to be wild
But will never be free

Beauty has called
And left her it all
She has no cares at all
In love with a dream

And he says he'll provide
When he makes her his bride
But she knows that it's lies
For he'll never cut it

But she wants to believe
So wants it to be
So she sits on his knee
She's the idiots' puppet

And the flowers bow their heads
And all the bluebells are dead
And the woodland is bare
All the leaves have been shed

The bitter north wind blows
The years come and go
She is but a shadow
Of what she could have been

And life's so inane
If she could just start again
Break free from these chains
But he keeps her so near

And he says he'll provide
When he makes her his bride
But she knows that it's lies
For he'll never cut it

But she wants to believe
So wants it to be
So she sits on his knee
She's the idiots' puppet

Her happiness devoid
Her dreams are destroyed
And he's still unemployed
And he keeps her so near

If he would just let her go
But it will never be so
So she puts on a show
For the idiot puppeteer

Such a sad little girl
So mad at the world
Such a sad little girl
In a sad little world

The Replica

Milton Keynes
The land of my dreams
With your H's and your V's
And your roundabouts

Milton Keynes
The land of my dreams
I wake up I scream
Let me out

Milton Keynes
The land of my dreams
You have a Point
But I cannot see it

Milton Keynes
The land of my dreams
With your Woods
And your Fields
Your Barns
And Parks
And Bridges
And Valleys
Your Walnut Trees
And Lakes...
Estates

Milton Keynes
The land of my dreams
How your Theatre District gleams
The gleaming sweat
On the shaven head
The beer belly
In the England vest
The British bulldog tattoo
The red white and blue
The Red Stripe and Special Brew
Buy three for two
Happy hour has never been so sad
When did things get this bad
In the land of my shattered dreams
But it's not just my Milton Keynes
It seems
That the whole of England's once green
And pleasant lands
Are now in the hands
Of the fat shaven headed tattooed man
In the football replica shirt

Shelter

When the city walls begin to melt
And the pavement starts to swelter
You shall breathe the cool crisp air
Deep inside my shelter

Sinking in the shifting sands
Caught on the helter-skelter
Sanctuary is close at hand
Deep inside my shelter

From the darkest corners of your mind
To the Mississippi Delta
All you seek you shall find
Deep inside my shelter

Mighty Oak Trees

They told me travel would broaden my mind
So I walked this lonely planet
Never sure of what I'd find
Or the secrets held within it
What mysteries the mighty oak trees
If only they had breath
Before the roars of chainsaws
Condemned them all to death
How quick the land has turned to sand
Where once the earth was lush
And instead of birds and whistling winds
Is now a deadly hush
So I set to sea to find myself
In a rented leaky boat
With an old stray dog for company
We just tried to stay afloat
Our throats were parched our rations low
As the sun beat down its rays
My faithful companion by my side
For eighty nights and days
Then he raised a paw
To a far-off shore
And I rowed towards the east
Then underneath a starlit sky
We hit upon the beach
Then dragged our bones over the stones
And settled for the night
Shivering cowering waking hourly
Something's just not right
When morning broke I filled the boat
With water fruit and fish
Working hard to catch the tide
As something was amiss

I combed the beach
I searched the trees
I climbed the highest peak
I looked for tracks upon the sand
And gazed far out to sea
I whistled high I whistled low
When it was time to leave
But what became of that old stray dog
I guess I'll never know
I sailed alone
I made it home
And took to my sick bed
With memories of old oak trees
And stray dogs in my head
I close my eyes I hear his cries
His howling at the moon
Calling for his only friend
And for him to sail back soon
I wake I scream this recurring dream
That does not fade with time
I set to sea to find myself
But instead I lost my mind
The years have passed I've sailed my last
And the old dog is surely dead
Like the memories of old oak trees
He's only in my head
But when the air is crisp and the moon is full
And the stars shine bright to morning
Turn your ear towards the East
And you will hear him calling

Your Eternal Sleep

I wandered out into the night
I stumbled through the rain
I had some time to kill
But I could not kill the pain
I've sold my soul to the bottle
But my heart is yours to keep
And we will meet again my love
In your eternal sleep

Take me to that magic place
Where the water falls
And I will see your pretty face
In the shallow pools
A blue lagoon
The silver moon
The coral of the deep
And I will see you soon my love
In your eternal sleep

Every dream we had is gone
What use is dreaming now?
I hold onto the tattered cards
That fates cruel hand has dealt
I've seen the suffering
Heard the screams
Enough to make you weep
But I will hold you once again
In your eternal sleep

How to Dump Your Boyfriend

I can see it in your eyes
I can hear it in your voice
Bullshit and lies
Your weapons of choice
Let the church bells ring out
Let all the saints rejoice
Let the heavens choir sing
And the angels go moist
I've made a decision
I've reached a conclusion
It's time to put an end
To your romantic delusions
No longer my accuser
No longer your bitch
So fuck off loser
It's time you were ditched

Late at Night

Late at night
The sky is black
A coronary
Heart attack
God gives life
Then takes it back
But I have lived with you

Yesterday
I got the sack
So I took my money
To the track
I lost it all
Then won it back
I'm so lost without you

I walk along
The polluted shore
And kick the shells up
From the war
And ask myself
What was it for
When I could have been with you

On a bench
On a pier
Distant memories
Far from here
Slowly fade
Then disappear
But I remember you

If I had
A single wish
All I'd ask
Was simply this
To touch her hair
And taste her kiss
Well perhaps a kiss or two

I cast my mind back
To the day
When my sweetheart
Slipped away
Just when I thought
She was here to stay
Please take me home with you

I think about her
Now and then
And know that we will
Meet again
It's just a case
Of where and when
When I will walk with you

So forgive me for
The grace I lack
The cards are dealt
We've cut the pack
I show the deuce
You turn the Jack
This debt is overdue

So late at night
The sky is black
A coronary
Heart attack
Just turn the key
And drop the latch
I'm coming home to you

The Born-Again Freedom Writer

The troubles of the world
Will not be solved by these words
They are one mans observations
But I demand that they be heard

Twisted in the smoking embers
Blackened by the fire
The Kalashnikov lies silent now
But this pen is still for hire

Democracy suppressed by greed
The noose is pulling tighter
Don't be a victim of what you read
Said the born-again freedom writer

Glad to Glasto

We sent our application
Then we waited for an age
But we never got a reply
From the Pyramid Stage
We sent them all our best work
Just like they said we should
And even if I do say so
It sounded pretty good

And we were glad to Glasto
But we never got the call
So sad that we can't go
Thanks for fuck all
It's a literary catastrophe
That we're not playing Glastonbury
But if that's how it has to be
Then thanks for fuck all

As the weeks went by with no reply
We started to despair
Another year of disappointment
Life is so unfair
I watched it on the telly
With a sense of rage
But in the solitude of my bedroom
The Poets take the stage

And we were glad to Glasto
But we never got the call
So sad that we can't go
Thanks for fuck all
So call the constabulary
Because we're not playing Glastonbury
And if you'd rather have Rick Astley
Well thanks for fuck all

Well I can't understand it
How we didn't get selected
It's just not how we planned it
I'm feeling all rejected
I really can't believe this
I'm phoning Michael Beavis
To ask if we can appear
At Glastonbury next year

And we were glad to Glasto
But we never got the call
So sad that we can't go
Thanks for fuck all
It's festival blasphemy
That we're not playing Glastonbury
It all seems very crass to me
Well thanks for fuck all

I don't mean to be defamatory
But we're not playing Glastonbury
And I don't mean this nastily
But thanks for fuck all

It's the depths of depravity
That we're not playing Glastonbury
More painful than a cavity
Thanks for fuck all

If girls could hear our poetry
They'd all want to sleep with me
But we're not playing Glastonbury
So thanks for fuck all

I'm crying in the lavatory
Because we're not playing Glastonbury
I've exhausted my vocabulary
Thanks for fuck all

And we were glad to Glasto
But we never got the call
So sad that we can't go
Thanks for fuck all

For One Night Only

She took the monster from my head
And with one sweet kiss she killed it dead
Not a single word between us said
I wore black and she wore red

We shared a smoke and nothing more
I told a joke she'd heard before
The perfumed sheets upon the bed
I wore black and she wore red

Daybreak brought the cleansing rain
We knew we'd never meet again
Returning home to those we wed
I wore black and she wore red

A Perfect Kiss

In silver moonlit layby land
He accidently brushed her hand
Nervously the couple stand
Looking at each other

No flowers will the young man send
Destined to stay just good friends
Is this how the story ends?
Perhaps they will be lovers

Many times such as this
A fleeting glance the chance is missed
Close your eyes and make a wish
The evening ends, a perfect kiss

If I only had a Pound

(for every time she said I love you, by now I wouldn't even have a pound)

She was the kind of girl
Who didn't need to try too hard
In fact...
She didn't need to try at all
She was out of this world
And out of my reach
And went out with every single boy in school
Except me
But I never will forget
The day that she said
Can you not do that please
Do you mind
Please can you not
Can you just stop
And naively I said 'what?'
And she said breathing
A little unkind
But I didn't mind
Because she spoke to me
And in my dreams
We walked hand in hand
Upon the sand
In paradise
In the promised land
And our footsteps
Never made a sound
And if I only had a pound
For every time she I love you
By now I wouldn't even have a pound
And if my life depended
On these three little words

Then by now I would be six feet underground
If I only had a pound

The years went by and up we grew
But I never knew
What happened to my dream girl
Although late at night
All alone
In my bed
In my head
I never will forget
The first time that she said
Can you not do that please
Do you mind
Can you not
And naively I said 'what?'
Then she'd softly whisper 'stop'
Don't stop
Do it some more
A feeling soft and warm
A feeling wet and warm
Upon the sheets
Two strangers on a desolate beach
Upon the sand
We'd walk hand in hand
To a sleepy little town
And there we'd settle down
And marry
Have three beautiful kids
Called Isabella and Sid
And Tyler
We'd get a cat
And a rottweiler
And everything those kids wanted
Those kids would surely have

We'd be the king and queen
The king and queen of chavs
And we all wear McKenzie hoodies
And back to front Burbary baseball caps
Oh wouldn't it be nice
It sounds like paradise
A paradise found
In our sleepy little town
If I only had a pound…
If I only had a pound
For every time she said I love you
By now I wouldn't even have a pound
And if my life depended
On these three little words
Then by now I would be six feet underground
If I only had a pound

My Bloody... Valentine

The table is set
The aperitifs poured
I've drawn the curtains
I've locked the doors
There is only you
There is only I
And forever you'll be
My bloody........................
Valentine

You're wearing that dress
It was my favourite you know
The one with the ribbons
The one with the bows
It's tattered and torn
With the test of time
But your beauty remains
My bloody..........................
Valentine

The day that we met
I knew you were the one
Our dreams had come true
Our reign had begun
I told you then
You would always be mine
And forever you'll be
My bloody..........................
Valentine

I heard a rumour
Through the grapevine
That the friends we once had
They all came to dine
On a banquet laced
With strychnine
And forever you'll be
My bloody.........................
Valentine

I'll raise you a glass
Of Bordeaux reserve'
The flesh in your mouth
Is all you deserve
So bloody and rare
This vulturine
And forever you'll be
My bloody.........................
Valentine

We live in the shadows
Avoid the light
I'll take you dancing
And party all night
Then return to our lair
Before the sunrise
And forever you'll be
My bloody.........................
Valentine

The centuries pass
We've seen them all
Dictatorships rise
The great empires fall
With you by my side
Not my concubine
And forever you'll be
My bloody........................
Valentine

The Boy from Albuquerque

Brian was a young man from Albuquerque
Who fell in love with an oven-ready turkey
He loved her smooth white tender skin
He basted her in butter and he massaged it in
He shaved her legs he clipped her wings
He made her bed in a roasting tin

Each day together was just fantastic
Brian had a thing about women in plastic
Bound and trussed with bits of elastic
And she even liked Christmas she was ecclesiastic

It wasn't long before they were going steady
She was plump and moist she was oven-ready
She didn't say much in fact not a word
But she liked a good stuffing she was his ideal bird
And his mates all came around when they first heard
Bearing gifts of an onion, potatoes and a fresh bunch of herbs

They were married on a hot summers' day in July
But they didn't go on honeymoon because turkeys don't fly
Upon the marital bed he turned to kiss her
But she'd lost her head she was all of a Twizzler
And that's when Brian noticed that all was not well
And that's when he noticed that terrible smell
Consumed by love he hadn't the heart to tell her
Was that a nasty little rash upon her smooth white skin
Was that... Salmonella!

Oh poor old Brian he hadn't a clue
So he sent for Doctor Bernard Matthews
Who immediately diagnosed avian bird flu
He said don't worry son I know just what to do

This terrible disease has spread from the coast
There's only one cure prepare the roast
I'll need garlic and rosemary and fennel and truffle
And carrots and parsnips and broccoli and brussels
As the oven door opened she screamed 'save me'
But Brian just smiled and stirred the gravy

He thought of her breast thigh leg and belly
And imagined them smothered in cranberry jelly
He gathered up her personal effects
As the family gathered to pay their respects
There were aunties and uncles some friends and a priest
They had all come around to join in the feast
And once the guests were suitably greeted
Brian ensured they were comfortably seated
And as they viewed her body she was dressed so neatly
As she lay on the table and whispered 'eat me'

Marcel Broadtheirs

These are the poems that will never be read
This is the prose that will never be said
Only discovered long after I'm dead
Yeah these are the poems that will never be read

These are the pages that will never be turned
These are the lessons that nobody learned
Faded from memory like a lover spurned
Yeah these are the pages that will never be turned

These are the thoughts that will never be aired
Lost in time because nobody cared
Entombed in cement like Marcel Broadtheirs
Yeah these are the thoughts that will never be aired

These are my footsteps beware you tread
These are the tears that will never be shed
Written in black or colitis red
Yeah these are my footsteps beware you tread

These are the poems that nobody read
Covered in dust under the bed
Up in the attic or down in the shed
Only discovered long after I'm dead

OK LJ

Ok LJ
Come and sit beside me baby
Let me tell you about the time
I used to dream that you would love me
Like you do
And you do

Well we've had good times
But it's true to say that lately
We have drifted our own separate ways
Our lives just seem so crazy
I miss you
And I do

And these old bones of mine
It's true they've seen some better times
Not sure I'll last much longer
But each day my love grows stronger
Love for you
My love for you

But one day soon
We're heading back to our lagoon
With no more bills to pay
We'll wash our troubles all away
Just me and you
Me and you

So hang on in their girl
For there's got to be a better world
Where our children come to play
I think I'm going there one day
And life is good
Life is good

So sit beside me LJ
And I'll tell you of my plan
I'm gonna turn the clocks back all the way
And I will be your man
My love is true
It's just for you

Well you may say that I'm a dreamer
But I swear that it's no lie
Just close your eyes my darling
And soon we'll hit the sky
We'll fly away
Let's go LJ

And here on my magic carpet
We will soar above the clouds
Until we find the secret island
That we used to talk about
When we were young
When love begun

And that night I sat and waited
Well I often reminisce
But who'd have thought that night would last
And lead us here to this
With just one kiss
A perfect kiss

The dark nights are drawing in
As the winter casts its net
But take my hand my darling
And we'll walk into a sun that never sets
It never sets
Never forget

Penultimate Poem

This is the penultimate poem
And in case you're unsure my friend
It's the one
Before the one
At the end

This is the penultimate poem
Alas it is regrettable
That the forty ninth of fifty
Is instantly forgettable

Just making up the numbers
Substitute for the reserves
The one before the one at the end
All original works

It's the valiant runner up
That never gets a mention
The penultimate is a troubled child
Held back in detention

The day before New Year's Eve
Or the fourth of November
The next one after Adan and Eve
That nobody remembers

The is the penultimate one
Easily forgotten
Like the other two Pistols
Neither Vicious nor Rotten

Perhaps...

This poem is not the longest
But that should not diminish it
Perhaps you will not sing along
Perhaps I'll never fin...

ABOUT THE AUTHOR

I have noticed a sharp increase in the number of bloggers, braggers and self-publicists during lockdown and choose not to join the growing list. As previously stated, there's not much worth knowing but I hope you found some enjoyment within these pages

Printed in Great Britain
by Amazon